DISC

D1177613

Date Due

CRICKETS AND FROGS

GRILLOS Y RANAS

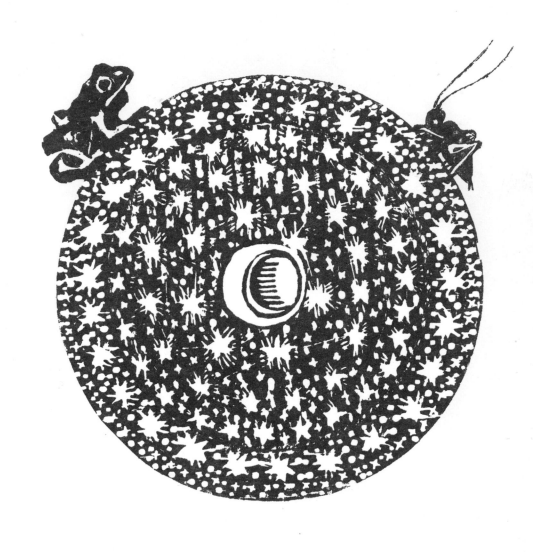

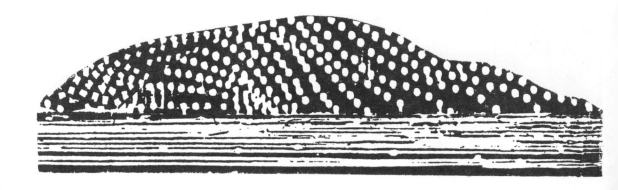

CRICKETS AND FROGS
A Fable by Gabriela Mistral

IN SPANISH AND ENGLISH

Translated and Adapted by Doris Dana

Illustrated by Antonio Frasconi

GRILLOS Y RANAS
Una Fábula de Gabriela Mistral

EN ESPAÑOL E INGLES

Traducción y Adaptación de Doris Dana

Ilustraciones de Antonio Frasconi

A Margaret K. McElderry Book

ATHENEUM 1972 NEW YORK

THE LIBRARY
CHILDREN'S LITERATURE COLLECTION
CALIFORNIA STATE UNIVERSITY HUMBOLDT
ARCATA, CALIFORNIA   95521

Text copyright © 1972 by Doris Dana
Illustrations copyright © 1972 by Antonio Frasconi
All rights reserved
Library of Congress catalog card number 72-77131
Published simultaneously in Canada by McClelland & Stewart, Ltd.
Manufactured in the United States of America
Printed by Connecticut Printers, Inc., Hartford
Bound by A. Horowitz & Son/Bookbinders, Clifton, New Jersey
First Edition

468
M 69/c
c. 1

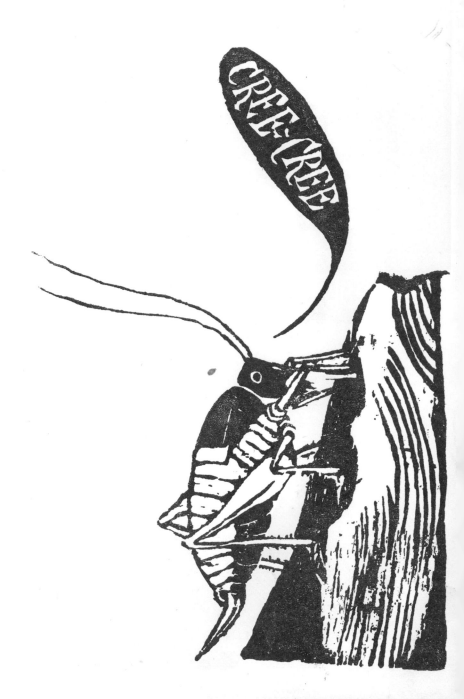

In the beginning there was only one Old Cricket in the gully. He chirped.

En el principio había un solo Viejo Grillo en la quebrada. Cantó.

Suddenly from a little patch of grass nearby came another chirp. Then another one, and again another. Soon the whole gully was chirping and singing. The song spilled out over the entire field and spread over the land with a great sweetness.

De pronto, de una hierba punzada por sus notas, fueron saliendo otros y otros. Unas noches después, cantaba la quebrada entera; más tarde llegaron al llano donde el canto extendido fué cobrando una gran suavidad.

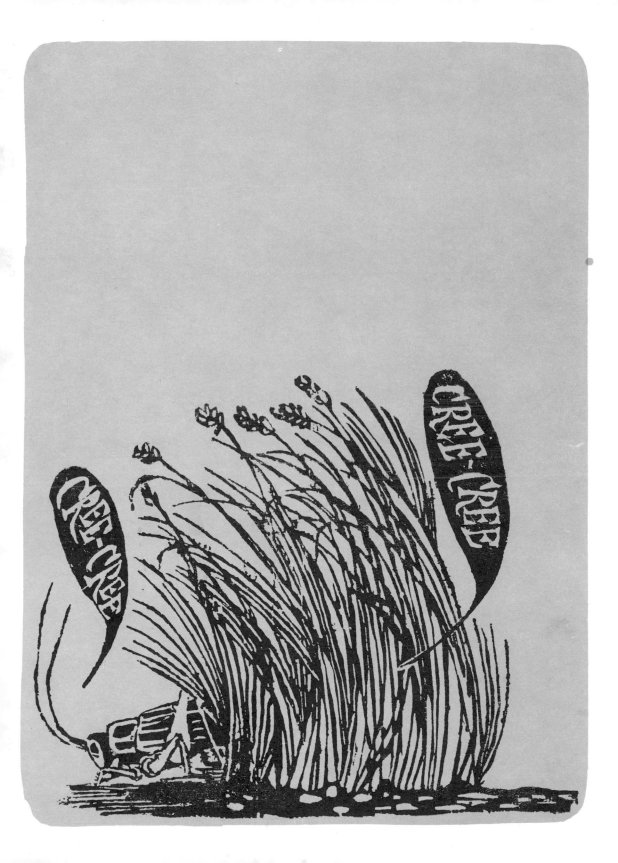

The Old Cricket became very worried. "Where am *I*?" he cried. "This cricket song is everywhere. Which song is *my* song? Which cricket am *I*?"

La desesperación del Viejo Grillo era ésta: ¿Dónde se encontraba él ahora, si cantaba en todas partes?

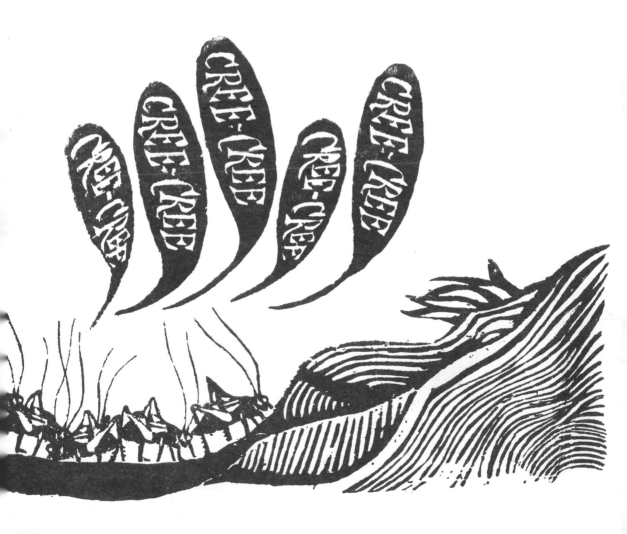

For a time everything grew very still and quiet in
the Old Cricket's kingdom. There was a long silence
that lasted many weeks.

Por un tiempo todo fué silencio y quietud en el dominio del Viejo Grillo. La calma duró varias semanas.

Then all at once a great croaking chorus of frogs shattered the stillness of night.

Pero de pronto un inmenso coro de ranas rompió la quietud de la noche.

As long as the ponds had been filled with clean pure water, the frogs were quiet. But when the water lilies, cattails, and bulrushes began to grow, the frogs started their song, and the night became alive with their croaking.

Mientras el agua de los estanques fué pura y límpida, las ranas no cantaban. Pero cuando los nenúfares, las espadañas, y los juncos invadieron sus aguas, empezó el canto malaventurado, y la noche vibró con su croar.

When the frogs stopped to rest their throats, the crickets started to chirp again more loudly than ever. The crickets and the frogs began a musical battle to see which could sing the loudest.

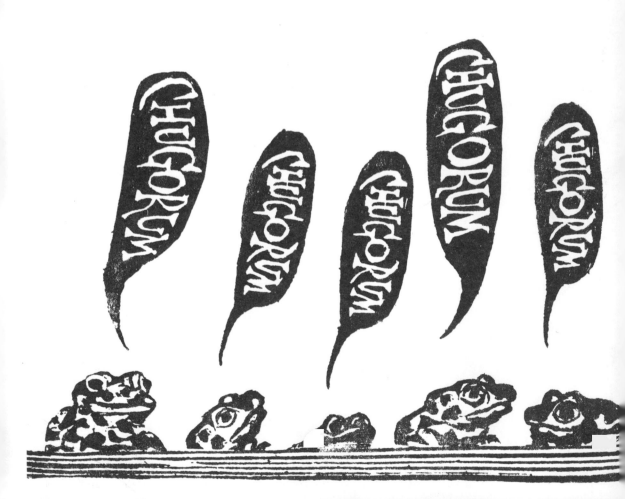

Cuando callaban para darle un descanso a sus gargantas, los grillos comenzaban su canto más fuerte que nunca. Fué así que empezó el duelo musical entre los grillos y las ranas para ver quien podía cantar más ruidosamente.

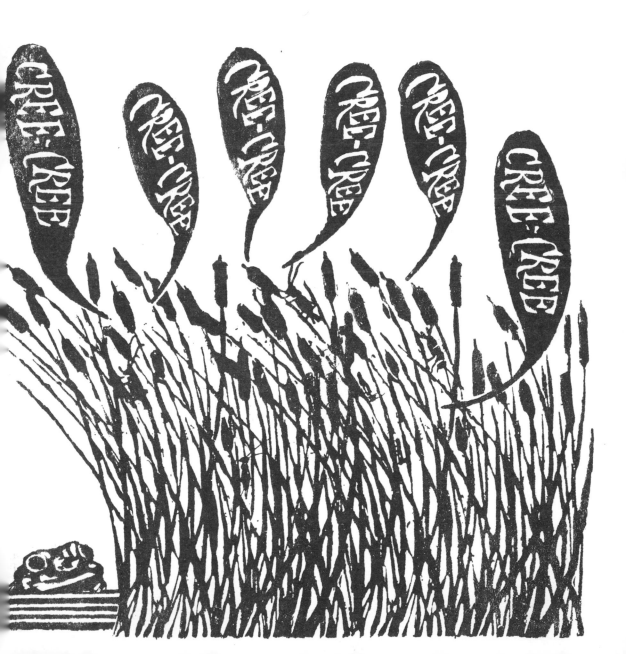

All the while the stars blinked down on them with approval. But which did the stars prefer? Were the stars blinking at the crickets or the frogs?

Se oía el desafío de las dos familias y las estrellas hacían su gran parpadeo de aprobación. ¿Pero a cuáles iba dirigida la aprobación?

It was a noisy battle. First one chorus sang out a
great rocking rhythm into the night. Then the other
began. Each one wanted the most silent part of the
night for his song.

El duelo era evidente. Uno de los coros se callaba
a causa del otro que se columpiaba en la noche.
Andaban disputándose el silencio.

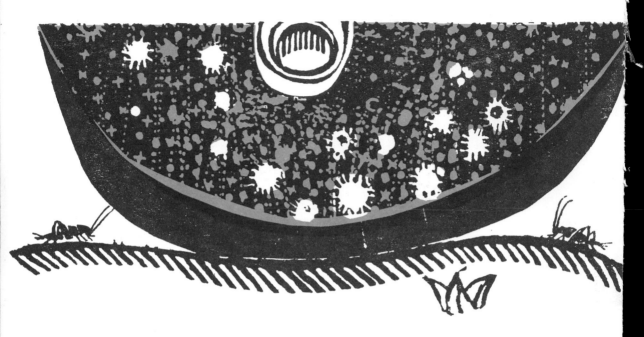

Finally the Old Cricket said: "Let us divide the night like a fruit, and each of us will sing for one half of the night." The crickets chose the most silent part of the night. So did the frogs. They could reach no agreement. From that day to this, they have *never* agreed.

El Viejo Grillo propuso a los sapos que partieran
la noche como una fruta y cantase cada pueblo
durante la mitad de ella. El obstáculo estuvo en que
ambos coros eligieron el más puro gajo de la noche,
y, hasta hoy, no hubo pacto.

And ever since, the Old Cricket keeps chirping:
"Where am *I*? Which cricket am *I*?" And all the
other crickets sing the same song: "Where am *I*?
Which cricket am *I*?"

Desde entonces el Viejo Grillo sigue cantando:
"¿Dónde estoy? ¿Cuál soy yo?" Y todos los grillos
cantan el mismo canto: "¿Dónde estoy? ¿Cuál
soy yo?"

From here to the starry sky you can hear the Old Cricket chirping everywhere. He will never again be ONE cricket – never again.

Y desde aquí hasta el cielo estrellado, se lo escucha por todas partes. No será UNO nunca más, nunca más.

GABRIELA MISTRAL was the first Latin American to receive the Nobel Prize for Literature. Born in a small village in the Andes mountains of Chile, she had no formal education after the age of eleven. Yet, self-taught, she became a teacher at the age of fourteen and went on to become the guiding force in the reforms of rural education in Latin America. She served in the League of Nations and later in the United Nations, and pioneered in establishing UNICEF. As the North American child delights in the stories of Hans Christian Andersen, so the Latin American loves the poems of Gabriela Mistral. Spanish-speaking children learn to read and write copying her verses, and on every playground from Mexico to Patagonia they join hands and dance their *rondas* while they sing the lyrics of her poems.

DORIS DANA, who has translated and adapted this fable, was a long-time friend of Gabriela Mistral. A poet and short-story writer, she has lectured extensively throughout Latin America. She was awarded the Order of Merit, the Chilean government's highest honor, for promoting better cultural understanding between the Americas. Her recently published book of translations, *Selected Poems of Gabriela Mistral,* was a significant literary event of 1971.

ANTONIO FRASCONI, one of the most forceful and poetic graphic artists of our time, has won many awards both here and abroad. His film *The Neighboring Shore,* using over one hundred woodcuts to illustrate the poems of Walt Whitman, won the Grand Prix at the Venice Film Festival in 1960. His works are in the collections of all major museums in the United States. Among his best-known multi-lingual books for children are: *See and Say, See Again, Say Again, The House That Jack Built,* and *The Snow and the Sun.*